ashlight

by **Betsy James**

trated by **Stacey Schuett**

I sit up   ur house

My sister is so little, she goes to sleep anywhere, even in restaurants. She doesn't care if we have to sleep in Grandpa's living room, or if Mom and Dad are far away, in the bedroom down the hall.

But all I can see is dark. That door to the hallway is a cave.

Out of my mouth comes a little crying sound.

Out of the cave comes a bear—but it's only Grandpa. "Did I hear my Mouse?" (My name's Marie, but Grandpa calls me Mouse.)

I rub my head on his warm pajama shirt.

"Dark, ain't it?" he says. "Thought you might like a flashlight."

He puts a heavy shape into my hands, and shows my fingers how to push the switch.

In the all-of-a-sudden light I see his
face, and Tibby sleeping.

"Now you're all right," he says. "If you
need me, you call."

The flashlight beam follows him back
down the hall.

I click the switch. The whole world disappears.

I click it again, quickly, and the world comes
jumping back. That forest of legs is the table.
That leaning mountain is the chair. Something
could hide there.

But wherever I point the flashlight, the shadows run away.

There is the cat teapot.

There is the blue bowl with peaches.

There is the music box that plays "The Tennessee Waltz," and there is the one-eyed horse that in the daytime I can ride.

The flashlight doesn't look at things all at once, the
way the sun does, but one by one. It's my night eye.

When I look in the mirror, I don't look like me.

I shake the flashlight. All the shadows shake.

Tibby sighs in her sleep, but doesn't wake.

A moth comes.
  Back and forth across the beam it
flies in flashes. The window screen is
crowded with whining midges,
bumbling June bugs, and ants with
wings. They love my light.

But I'm the one who chooses when it shines. I can cover it with one hand. Watch!

The flashlight's warm. Fire glows right through my bones.

I can go into dark places, shining.

My sheet is a tent. I'm hunting
treasure. Here are my jewels. There
are bears!

"Tibby!" they growl. "Eat Tibby!"

But I tame them like moths.
"Stay there, you bears!" I say,
and they stay.

I explore to the very bottom of the bed,
where it's usually just feet.
Through caves and tunnels I crawl back
out to the cool air.

The living room
is new. This is my
flashlight country.
I make the sun
shine here. I can
make shadows run.
I can boss moths
and bears. I am
the queen of the
night world,
Marie! I can see in
the dark.

I switch off the light.

I switch it on again, but the shadows are back.

They move. Tibby sleeps.

"Grandpa?"

He comes out of the dark, rumpling his hair. "What, Mouse?"

"Nothing. I was making sure."

"Sure."

After he goes, I whisper, "Don't be scared, Tibby. I've got a flashlight."

http://www.randomhouse.com/

Library of Congress Cataloging-in-Publication Data

James, Betsy.
Flashlight / by Betsy James ; illustrations by Stacey Schuett.
p.   cm.
Summary: Marie is afraid to sleep overnight in her grandparents' living room
until her grandfather gives her a flashlight so that she can see in the dark.
ISBN 0-679-87970-6 (trade) — ISBN 0-679-97970-0 (lib. bdg.)
[1. Fear of the dark—Fiction. 2. Grandfathers—Fiction.] I. Schuett, Stacey, ill.
II. Title.
PZ7.J15357F1   1997
[E]—dc20   95-33333

Printed in Singapore

10 9 8 7 6 5 4 3 2 1